The
Little Red
Hen

A Classic Fairy Tale
Illustrated by Camille Semelet

· Abbeville kids ·

A Division of Abbeville Publishing Group

New York · London · Paris

Once upon a time there was a little red hen who lived all alone in her little house.

Not far from there, on top of a hill among some rocks, lived a sly fox. The fox, always hungry, sat outside his den and dreamed day and night of catching the little red hen.

"She must be so tender!" he thought. "I'd love to cook her in my big pot. What a great supper my old mother and I would have!"

But he knew it would not be easy to catch the little red hen. She was too smart and too careful.

Every time she left the house, she would lock
the door and take the key. When she came home,
she would carefully lock the door behind her
and put the key in her apron pocket, with her
scissors, needle, and thread.

But one day, the fox finally thought of a way
to catch her.

He left early in the morning, saying to his old mother:

"Fill the big pot and put it on the stove; we're going to eat the little red hen for supper." He took a big bag, ran to the little hen's house, and waited.

Soon, the little red hen stepped out and, without

locking the door, she started to gather some sticks to light her fire.

The fox slid behind a pile of wood. While she was bent over, he slipped into the house and hid behind the door.

When the little red hen went inside and turned to lock the door—Oh! She saw the fox with his big bag wide open to catch her.

The little red hen was terribly frightened!

But she didn't panic. She flew to the top of the
cupboard, and cried to the nasty fox:

"You haven't caught me yet!"

"We'll see about that," said the fox.

And what do you think he did?

He stood right below the little red hen and began
to spin, round and round, running after his tail,
faster, and faster, and faster.

The spinning made the poor little red hen dizzy,
and she lost her balance and fell right into the
big bag, which the fox had left open on the floor.

He snatched up the bag and left to return to his den and the big pot.

The long, steep hill tired him out. He stopped for a moment to rest and soon fell asleep. Once he stopped, the little red hen's head stopped spinning too, and she got to work.

First, she took her scissors out of her pocket, and
CLIP! cut a little hole in the bag to peek through.
Then CLIP! CLIP! she opened the bag and slipped out.
She put a big rock in the bag, and quickly, quickly
sewed it up again with her needle. Then she hid
as fast as she could.

When the fox woke up, he set off again, with
the rock in his bag. He said to himself:

"This little red hen is so heavy! I didn't think
she was so fat. She'll make a great meal!"

On he trudged, and finally he arrived at his den.

As soon as his mother saw him, she called out:

"Do you have the little red hen?

"Yes, yes," he said. "Is the water hot?"

"It's boiling away," said his old mother.

"Careful, now, take the lid off the pot. I'll dump the hen inside. Make sure that she doesn't fly away."

The old mother fox lifted the lid off the pot.

The fox opened the bag, grabbed one end, and shook the bag over the pot.

Splash! The big rock fell into the pot, and the pot overflowed on the fox and his old mother. They ran away, and no one ever saw them again.

And the little red hen went back to her little house, where she lived happily and safely ever after.

Look carefully at these pictures from the story.
They're all mixed up. Can you put them back
in the right order?

a

c

b

d

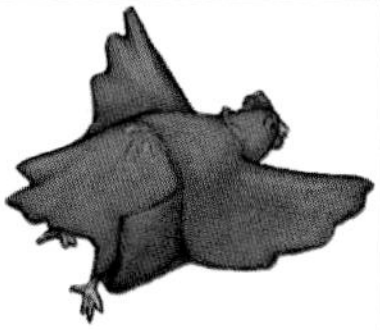

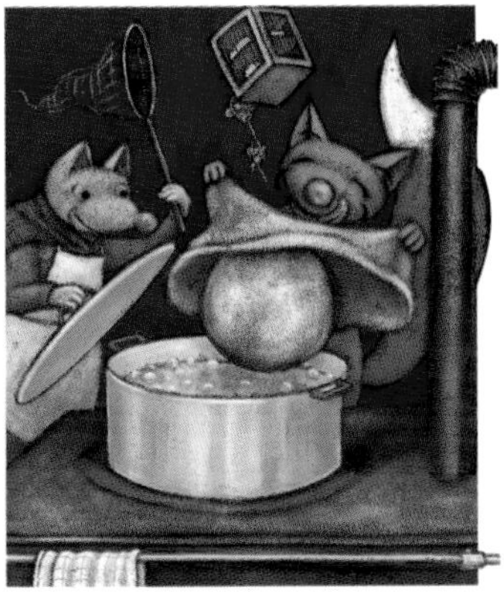

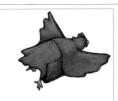

e

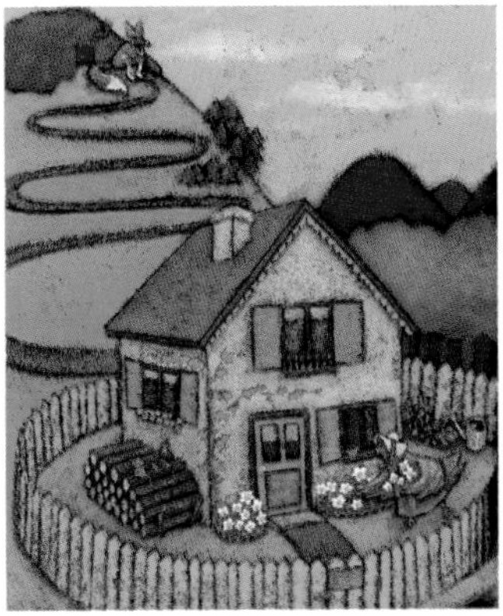

f

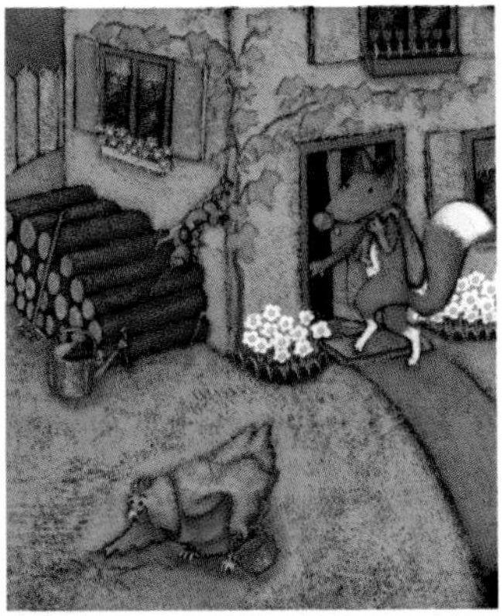

g

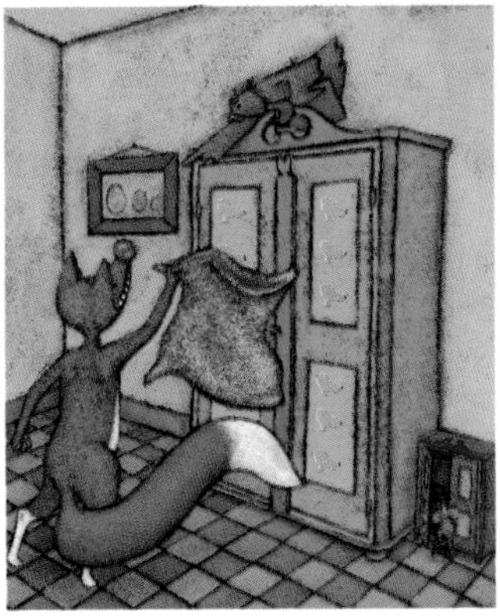

h

Correct order: f, d, g, a, h, b, e, c